Home Alone

Adapted by **Mark Mayerson**

Edited by **Paul Kropp**

Based on the screenplay by
Deborah Jarvis *and* **Anita Kapila**

Graphics by **Studio 345**

Monster By Mistake Theme Song

Hi my name is Warren and I'm just
a kid like you,

Or I was until I found evil
Gorgool's magic Jewel.

Then he tricked me and I read
a spell, now every
time I sneeze,

Monster By
Mistake…

My sister Tracy tries the
Spell Book. She
never gets it right.

But Tracy doesn't ever give
up, 'cause you know one day
she might

Find the words that will
return me to my former width
and height.

I'm a Monster By Mista….ah….ah…

I'm gonna tell you 'bout Johnny the ghost,

He's a wisecracking, trumpet playing friend.

He lives up in the attic (shhh…Mom and Dad don't know)

Johnny always has a helping hand to lend.

My secret Monster-iffic life always keeps me on the run.

And I have a funny feeling that the story's just begun.

Everybody thinks it's pretty awesome I've become

A Monster By Mistake!

I'm a Monster By Mistake!

I'm a Monster By Mistake!

Monster by Mistake
Text © 2002 by Winding Stair
Graphics © 2002 by Monster by Mistake Enterprises Ltd.
Monster By Mistake Created by Mark Mayerson
Produced by Cambium Entertainment Corp. and Catapult Productions
Series Executive Producers: Arnie Zipursky and Kim Davidson

All rights reserved. The use of any part of this publication reproduced, transmitted in any form or by any means, electronic, mechanical, photocopying, recording or otherwise, or stored in a retrieval system, without prior written consent of the publisher is an infringement of the copyright law. In the case of photocopying or other reprographic copying, a license from the Canadian Copyright Licensing Agency (CANCOPY) may be obtained.

National Library of Canada Cataloging in Publication Data

Mayerson, Mark
Home alone

(Monster by mistake ; 2)
Based on an episode of the television program, Monster by mistake.
ISBN 1-55366-211-3

I. Jarvis, Deborah, 1954– II. Kapila, Anita III. Kropp, Paul, 1948— IV. Cambium Film & Video Productions Ltd. V. Monster by mistake (Television program) V. Title. VI. Series: Mayerson, Mark Monster by mistake ; 2.

PS8576.A8685H65 2002 jC813'.6 C2002901102-7
PZ7.M39H65 2002

Winding Stair Press
An imprint of Stewart House Publishing Inc.
290 North Queen Street, #210
Etobicoke, Ontario, M9C 5K4 Canada
1-866-574-6873

Executive Vice President and Publisher: Ken Proctor
Director of Publishing and Product Acquisition: Susan Jasper
Production Manager: Ruth Bradley-St-Cyr
Copy Editing: Martha Campbell
Text Design: Laura Brady
Cover Design: Darrin Laframboise

This book is available at special discounts for bulk purchases by groups or organizations for sales promotions, premiums, fundraising and educational purposes. For details, contact: Stewart House Publishing Inc., Special Sales Department, 195 Allstate Parkway, Markham, Ontario L3R 4T8. Toll free 1-866-474-3478.

1 2 3 4 5 6 07 06 05 04 03 02

Printed and bound in Canada by Transcontinental

COLLECT THEM ALL

1 Monster By Mistake

2 Home Alone

3 Entertaining Orville

4 Kidnapped

5 Tracy's Jacket

6 Gorgool's Pet

7 Fossel Remains

8 Billy Caves In

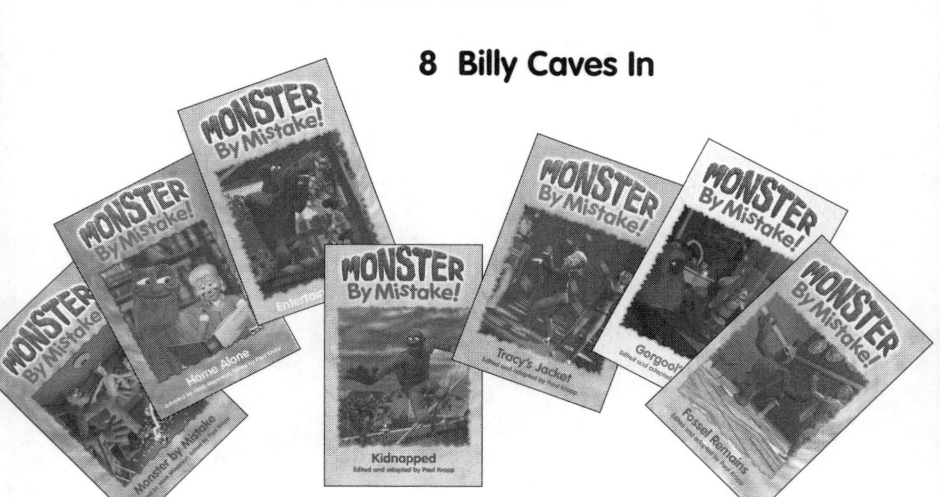

Contents

Chapter 1

Warren Patterson was in for a different kind of evening. His parents were going out and his sister, Tracy, was going to be left in charge. Also, he turned into a large blue monster when he sneezed.

Warren just hoped that Tracy would be better than their last babysitter. That girl had treated them both like little kids. She bossed them around and told them what shows they could watch on TV. And she didn't even read

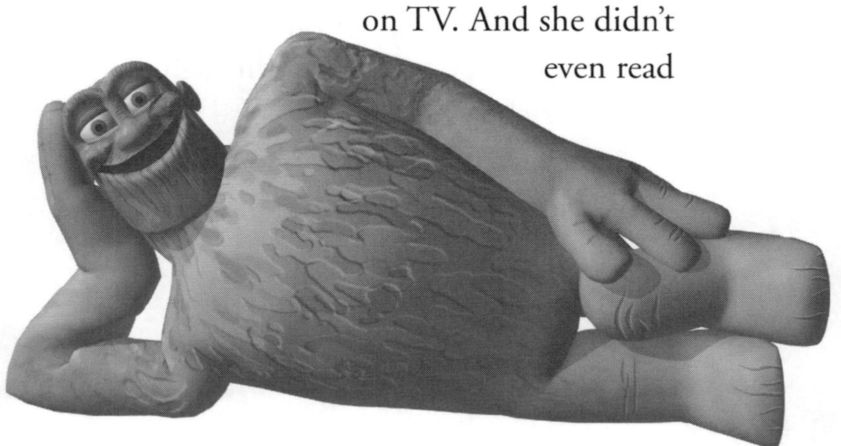

them a bed-time story!

Warren was pretty sure that Tracy would do a better job than that. She had to. Their parents were going out to some concert, and Tracy was the only sitter they could find.

Warren sighed. He could hear his father shouting to his mom from the foot of the stairs. "Come on, Roz! We're going to be late!"

"Better hurry, Mom," said Tracy. "You don't want to be late for Umberto Ungulessi. He may never come to Pickford for a concert again."

Their mother came down the stairs, dressed for the big evening out. She looked at Tracy and went through her babysitter checklist.

"Tracy, do you have the phone number of the Pickford Palace dinner theater?"

"Got it," Tracy replied.

"The Mumfords next door?"

"Yes, 555-1543."

"All the emergency numbers. . . the police and fire department?"

"Got 'em."

"The number for Warren's allergy doctor?"

Tracy rolled her eyes. "I can look it up! *Mom*, I've babysat before!"

Tracy was 12 now, almost a teenager, but her parents still treated her like a kid. That wasn't fair. Tracy knew she was smart and capable. She could take care of anything. . . except getting Warren cured of his monster problem.

Tom Patterson was in a hurry to get going. A big storm had been predicted for that night, and Tom wanted to be in the theater before it started. He kept looking at his watch while his wife put on makeup.

"We told your Aunt Dolores you'd be home alone," he said. "She may look in on you."

"Aunt Dolores doesn't have to, Dad.

I'm in charge!" Tracy announced.

"I suppose," said her father, "but there's nothing like having a police officer in the family just in case there's any trouble."

Just before getting her coat, their mother handed a videotape to Warren. Warren expected a nice family cartoon

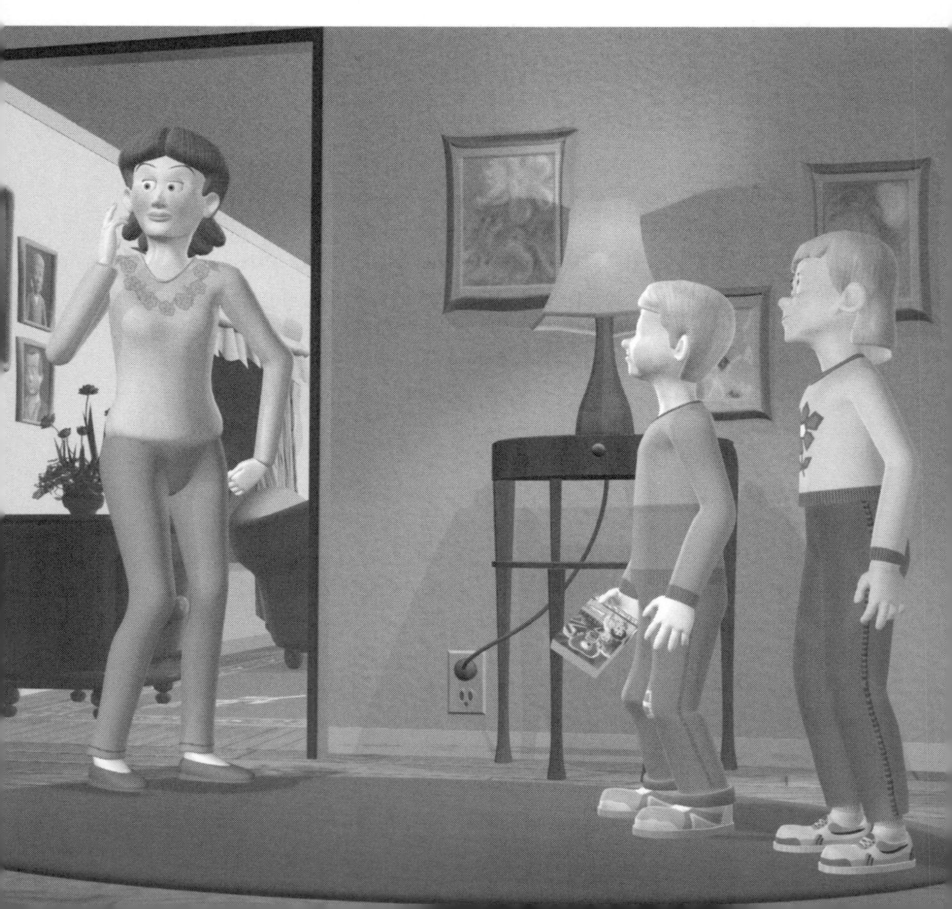

movie. Instead, he got *The Swamp Monster That Ate Alabama.*

Warren and Tracy exchanged a look.

"Uh, Mom, are you trying to tell us something?" Tracy asked.

"Oh, not really," their mom said. "I know how much you like monsters, Warren, so I rented it for you. I loved this film when I was your age. But if you get too scared, just turn it off and go to bed." Their mom smiled and walked away.

Warren shook his head. If his mom thought a movie monster was scary, she should see what happened when *he* sneezed. Rumors were flying all around town about "the Pickford monster." Everybody was scared, but the Patterson kids knew that the monster wouldn't hurt anyone. In fact, the monster was just Warren – big, blue and a bit scary – but just Warren.

"Hey, guys," Warren and Tracy heard from over their heads. They looked up to see Johnny the ghost wearing a bow tie. Johnny was the friendly ghost who lived in the attic, though he kept himself invisible to the older Pattersons.

"What's the occasion?" asked Tracy.

"Umberto Ungulessi is one of my favorite singers, too," said Johnny. "I'm going to tag along with your parents tonight."

"You mean I'm stuck here with Tracy, all alone?"

"Sorry, guy, but I can't pass up a concert like this. Catch you later," said Johnny. He quickly vanished before their eyes.

Warren was facing an interesting night. A strange old horror movie, his sister babysitting. . . and this awful allergy. "Oh no," Warren groaned. He could feel the sneeze coming on.

"Ah . . . ah . . . ah-choo!"

With a sudden sizzle and a flash of light, Warren turned into the Monster.

He and Tracy looked at each other. They were both worried that their parents would stumble upon Warren's secret.

"Was that you sneezing, Warren?" called their mother.

"No," the Monster called back to her. Fortunately, his voice stayed the same even when his body got big. "It was Tracy talking about this new band, the Ahchoos. I think they're Irish."

Tracy shook her head. "Quick, Warren, sneeze again and turn back to a kid! They're coming!"

But Warren always found it hard to make himself sneeze –

even with an allergy. He tried, rubbing his nose, but it just wasn't working. Both of them could hear their mother's steps. Finally, Tracy grabbed some dust from the stairs and threw it in his face.

"Ah . . . ah . . . ah-choo!"

Warren was himself again, just as his mother came through the door. "Be sure to give Warren his new allergy medicine, Tracy. Maybe this will help with that sneezing problem of his."

"I can take it myself," Warren told her.

"I know, dear, but your sister is in charge tonight."

Warren groaned. Tracy went to the door and waved goodbye to their parents.

"Just remember what Mom said," Tracy told her brother. "I'm in charge, whether you're the monster or just you! Leave everything to me and we'll have no problems at all."

Chapter 2

None of the Pattersons could see the two figures who were crouching by the side of the house. One was very large: an unshaven man with a large jaw and very large ears. The other was tiny: a small blue creature trapped inside a clear ball.

"The parents are gone, Master," the giant said.

He was holding the clear ball carefully. Inside it, the blue creature named Gorgool rubbed his hands together.

The moonlight glinted off the horn that grew out of his forehead.

"We've just had some stupendous luck," said Gorgool. "The parents have gone out for the night. That means those stupid children are home alone. If there was ever a chance to get the jewel and the *Book of Spells*, tonight is it!"

"So?" asked his servant, who was very loyal, but not too bright.

"So then we can cast the spell that frees me from this accursed ball!" yelled Gorgool. "Take me around to the back of the house. We're going to do a little spying."

Inside the house, Tracy was pouring Warren's allergy medicine. Warren wrinkled his nose. He swallowed the spoonful quickly, but couldn't help making a face.

"Is the medicine working?" asked Tracy.

Warren sneezed quickly three times.

Just as quickly, he changed back and forth from boy to monster. When he stopped sneezing, he was the Monster . . . but he still had a tickly nose.

"I guess not," said Tracy.

"Who cares?" said the Monster. "I can stay a monster all night if I want. There's nobody to see me but you. Let's go watch the movie!"

Tracy had another idea. There was a magic spell that she had wanted to try, but it was risky if her parents were home. Tonight was her chance! She explained all this to Warren, who had little choice but to go along. After all, Tracy was in charge.

The two of them went up to Tracy's room. Tracy carefully took the Jewel of

Fenrath and the *Book of Spells* out of the chest at the foot of her bed.

"Ick merka fekorum," chanted Tracy. *"Bernoulli vola lifto stem mercado aviana stileta winola flecka!"* The Jewel of Fenrath started to glow. Suddenly, a blue lightning bolt came out of the jewel. It zoomed around the room, looking for the target of its magic. And then . . . it hit Tracy!

In the backyard, Gorgool and his

servant gazed up at Tracy's bedroom window. They could see the flashing glow from the jewel.

"They're using it! The Jewel of Fenrath!" said Gorgool. "Get up there now and take it from them. And get the *Book of Spells*!"

The servant was nervous as he stared up at the second-storey window. He was large and strong, but he was very afraid of heights. "Up there?" he whined.

"Yes, you fool," Gorgool shouted. "Quickly, quickly! The children don't matter. Just get the book and the jewel. That's what we need!"

Chapter 3

Up in Tracy's bedroom, the blue lightning had delivered its spell. Tracy Patterson began rising off the floor. Without any effort at all, she was rising like a helium balloon.

"I'm flying, Warren! I'm flying!"

"I can see. I can see," the Monster replied, staring as his sister rose to the ceiling.

Tracy flew around her room, but her flying was clumsy. She bumped her head on the ceiling. Then she bounced against a bookcase and almost knocked over the goldfish bowl.

"I'll need some time to get the hang of this," she said.

Her brother was not impressed. Almost every time Tracy tried a spell, something

seemed to go wrong. Tonight she was an out-of-control Peter Pan. The Monster could only shake his very large head.

"Let's go watch the movie," said the Monster, as he headed downstairs.

Tracy flew after him, bumping into the door frame on the way out. By the time she reached the bottom of the stairs, she was flying with more confidence.

The Monster popped the video into the VCR and sat down. The sound of a scream and dramatic music filled the room as the movie started.

"I can't believe Mom actually liked this," said the Monster.

"She was just a kid," Tracy explained.

"Well, I'm just a kid and I think this is awful," her brother replied. On the screen, the swamp monster was already eating a city bus.

"Hey, how about we make some popcorn before the swamp guy gets a stomach ache?"

"Good idea," replied the Monster. "Popcorn can make even a bad movie a little bit better."

Tracy smiled as she flew towards the kitchen. She was so busy looking for the popcorn maker that she didn't see the two shapes out in the backyard.

"Start climbing!" commanded Gorgool.

His servant was busy stacking garbage

cans on top of each other. Gorgool had ordered him to climb up to Tracy's bedroom where the Jewel of Fenrath had been glowing.

The servant climbed onto the cans and tried to keep his balance as they wobbled. He was very scared of heights. He was afraid he'd fall off and get hurt. And he still couldn't reach the window.

"What are you waiting for?" demanded Gorgool. "Jump inside!"

The servant jumped and barely reached the sill. He hung by his fingertips, terrified. At last, with a lot of huffing and puffing, he was able to pull himself up. There, on the floor in front of him, was the jewel!

He reached through the window and had his hand on the jewel when a crack of thunder startled him. "Oh, oh, OH!" he cried. Then he lost his balance and fell to the ground.

Tracy and the Monster were in the kitchen making popcorn. They heard the noise of the servant falling and the garbage cans rolling.

"Did you hear that?" asked Tracy.

"It was thunder, I think," said the Monster, nervously. Warren might be the size of a giant, but that didn't make him any braver than he was as a boy.

"That must be it," said Tracy. "The forecast said it was supposed to rain."

Tracy tried to sound calm so her brother wouldn't be scared, but Tracy was worried. What if some thief was trying to break into the house? What would they do then?

Out in the yard, the servant was flat on his back on the grass. "Oh, oh, oh noooo!"

Gorgool was perched on a garbage-can lid that was balanced on a fallen can like a teeter-totter. "Stop moaning, you fool," he ordered.

"The thunder scares me, Master," replied the servant.

"Did you get the jewel?" asked Gorgool.

"I had my fingers right around it, but . . . but . . ."

"You let it go?" screamed Gorgool. "Idiot. Imbecile! You have ruined every chance we've ever had to get the jewel back!"

"I'm sorry, Master."

"Sorry is useless, you dimwit," Gorgool sputtered. He fumed silently for a second, and then burst out with anger, "You're fired!"

The servant was shocked. Fired? How could he be fired? He had been Gorgool's

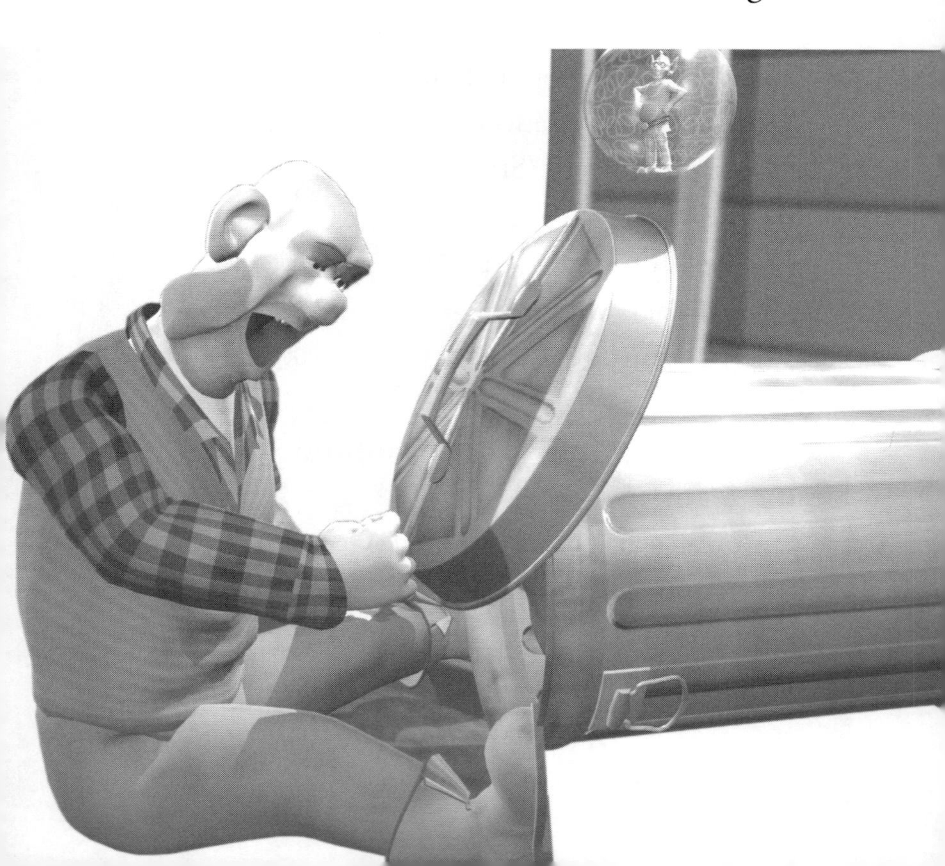

servant for as long as he could remember – at least a month or two. What would he do without Gorgool?

"I'll try again, Mighty Gorgool," said the servant. "I'll climb right back up. I will. I will."

"I'm through with you," said Gorgool. "I'll get the jewel back on my own. I don't need a dunderhead like you holding me back."

"Please, Master," begged his servant. "I'll do better from now on. I'll be smarter, really I will. I promise!"

For emphasis, the servant slammed his fist down on the garbage-can lid. Besides making a thunderous noise, the force of his blow sent Gorgool shooting into the air!

Chapter 4

Gorgool sailed up and through Warren's bedroom window on the second floor. The servant looked up and realized what he had done.

"Don't worry, Master! I'll save you!" he shouted.

The servant scratched his head, trying to figure out some way to get up to the window. He had to rescue Gorgool to get his job back, but what? As he paced, he had the beginning of an idea.

Unfortunately, the rest of the idea didn't come to him that quickly. Still, he kept pacing . . . and thinking . . . and pacing until he tripped over a ladder.

"Stupid ladder! You made me forget my idea! Now I'll never figure out a way to climb up to that . . ."

The servant blinked his eyes a few times and then broke into a grin. He had suddenly figured out the obvious.

"Hey, I could use the ladder!"

Quickly, the servant leaned the ladder against the house. He was just about to climb up when he heard footsteps. He dashed around to the side of the house to hide.

In the darkness, a shadowy figure pointed a flashlight around the yard. After not finding anything, the figure shut off the flashlight and moved away.

Up in Warren's room, a wobbly Gorgool was rolling around Warren's bed. As he looked around, his eyes came to rest on Warren's toy tank. Gorgool's face lit up at the sight.

"Yes! My vehicle! My army!"

Gorgool rolled his ball off the bed and onto the top of the tank. When he landed, he accidentally pushed a button that made the turret spin around. Soon he was figuring out how to use all the buttons.

Down in the kitchen, Tracy wondered about the sound over her head.

"Did you hear that?" she asked her brother.

"I think it came from my bedroom," said the Monster.

Up above their heads, Gorgool shifted his ball to hit a button. The tank moved forward, slamming into a door frame.

"There it goes again," said Tracy. Now she was a little scared.

“M-maybe we better check it out,” said the nervous Monster. “I guess I should go because I’m b-b-bigger.”

“No, I’ll check it out,” said Tracy. “I’m the babysitter!”

Tracy floated towards the hall with the Monster following behind her. Suddenly, the phone rang, making them both jump.

“It’s just the phone,” said Tracy, as she flew over to get it. It was their mother calling.

“Hi, Mom. No, everything’s fine,” said Tracy. “We’re just having some popcorn and watching that movie. Funny noises? Oh, that’s just the movie, Mom. Don’t worry. Everything is under control.”

The Monster could barely keep a straight face as he listened to his sister lying on the phone. Under control? Tracy was flying. He was in his monster shape. There was a strange noise from upstairs. And now he could see a dark shape outside the window!

"Tracy," he whispered. "Somebody's coming across the backyard."

"Mom, look, we're fine. Everything is A-OK," Tracy said, as her mother rambled on.

"Tracy," the Monster whispered. "It's coming closer!"

Tracy tried to look through the window, but it was hard from where she was floating.

"Listen, Mom. Don't worry. Go back and enjoy the concert. No problems here, Mom."

"No problems!" the Monster whispered, trying to keep his voice under control. "There might be a monster out there!"

That would make two monsters, Tracy thought to herself. If only she could get her mother off the phone, she might be able to deal with the one outside.

"Can you see what it is?" whispered Tracy.

The Monster shook his head.

Suddenly, the yard was lit up by a bolt of lightning. There, outside the kitchen window, holding a flashlight, was Aunt Dolores.

The Monster and Tracy screamed with surprise.

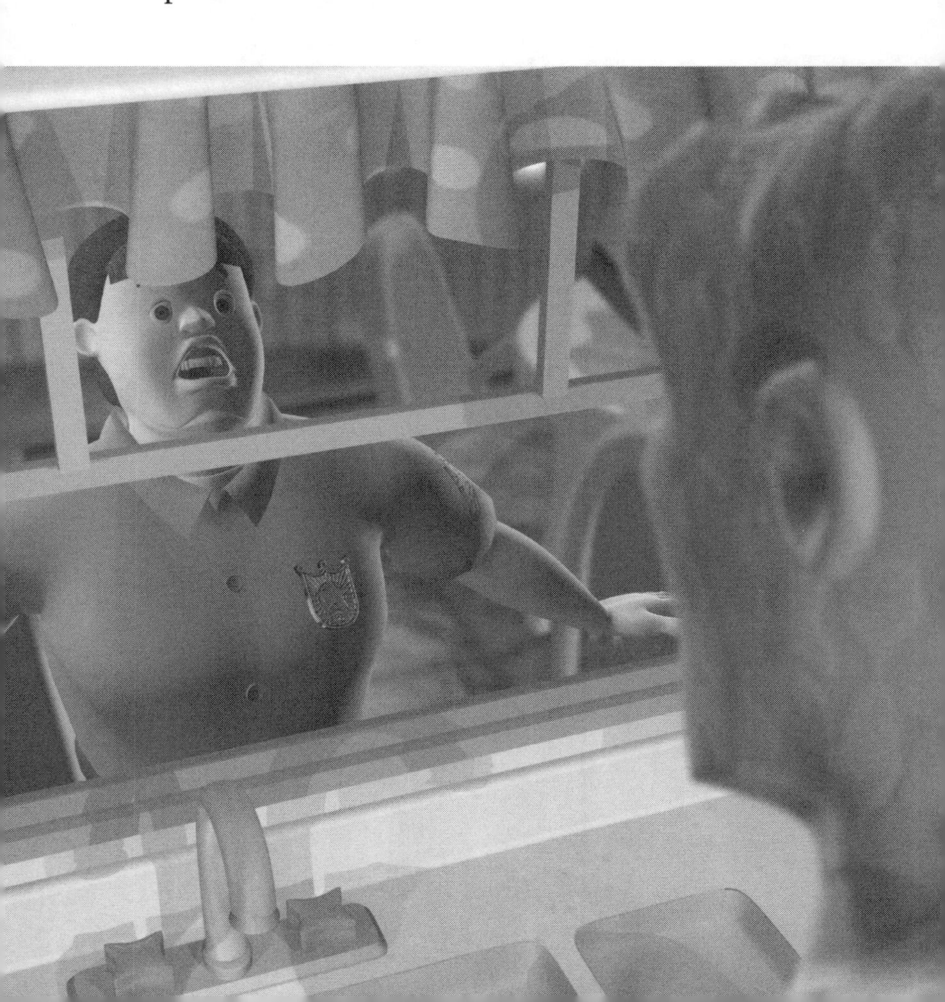

Aunt Dolores screamed, too! Right in front of her eyes was the giant Pickford monster!

Chapter 5

"Tracy! Warren! It's your Aunt Dolores! Stay calm! I'll save you!" yelled Dolores from the backyard.

"She saw you!" Tracy whispered to her brother. Then she turned her attention back to the phone.

"No, Mom. That wasn't a scream. It's just . . . Aunt Dolores is here. Listen, I have to go now. Have a good time." Tracy hung up the phone.

The doorknob rattled. Aunt Dolores was trying to get in.

"Monster!" Aunt Delores shouted into the house. "As assistant chief of the Pickford Police, I'm ordering you to release those children! Come out with your hands up."

“What are we going to do?” asked the Monster.

“You’ve got to sneeze! Right now!” said Tracy. She flew over and grabbed a pepper shaker. In a flash, she started shaking pepper onto her brother’s monster nose.

"It's not working!" whined the Monster. "It must be that new allergy medicine."

"We're going to be toast if she finds us like this!" Tracy declared.

"Worse than toast," the Monster declared. "Bread crumbs, little blue bread crumbs!"

Outside, Aunt Dolores got a running start and aimed herself at the back door. The whole house shook when she connected.

"She'll break the door down!" said the Monster.

"I guess I better let her in," said Tracy. She tried to get her feet on the floor, but she kept floating up. No matter how hard she tried, she couldn't get back to the floor. Finally, she grabbed a chair and forced herself down.

"Stand back, kids! I'm coming in!" yelled Aunt Dolores from the backyard.

"Quick," said Tracy to her brother. "Open the door and then hide in the basement."

The Monster opened the door and just made it to the basement before Dolores came barreling in. Naturally, she fell flat on her face and slid across the kitchen floor.

"Oh, Aunt Dolores! Hi!" said Tracy, trying hard to sound normal.

"Where is he? Where's the Pickford monster?" demanded Dolores as she jumped to her feet.

"I didn't see any monster," said Tracy. "Are you feeling all right, Aunt Dolores? You had a nasty fall. Maybe you're seeing things."

"He was here in this very kitchen," replied Aunt Dolores. "Wait a sec, where's Warren?"

'He's . . . around . . . uh, somewhere," said Tracy.

"Holy Canoly!" yelled Aunt Dolores. "The monster's got your brother!"

With that, Dolores ran out of the kitchen and up to the second floor. Barreling into Warren's room, she called his name, but no one answered.

"Don't worry, sweetie, I'll find you! Nothing gets past this member of Pickford's finest!" Dolores ran from Warren's room and continued to explore.

Gorgool drove the toy tank out from under Warren's bed. "Nothing gets past Pickford's finest, eh?" chuckled Gorgool. "We'll see about that."

Gorgool drove the tank into the hallway and then into Tracy's room. There, on the floor in front of him, was the thing he wanted most.

"Finally!" gloated Gorgool in triumph. "The Jewel of Fenrath! In a moment I'll be free. Then the world will feel the wrath of Gorgool!"

Chapter 6

Gorgool had a problem. How could he pick up the Jewel of Fenrath when he was stuck inside his ball? The spell was useless unless he had control of the jewel.

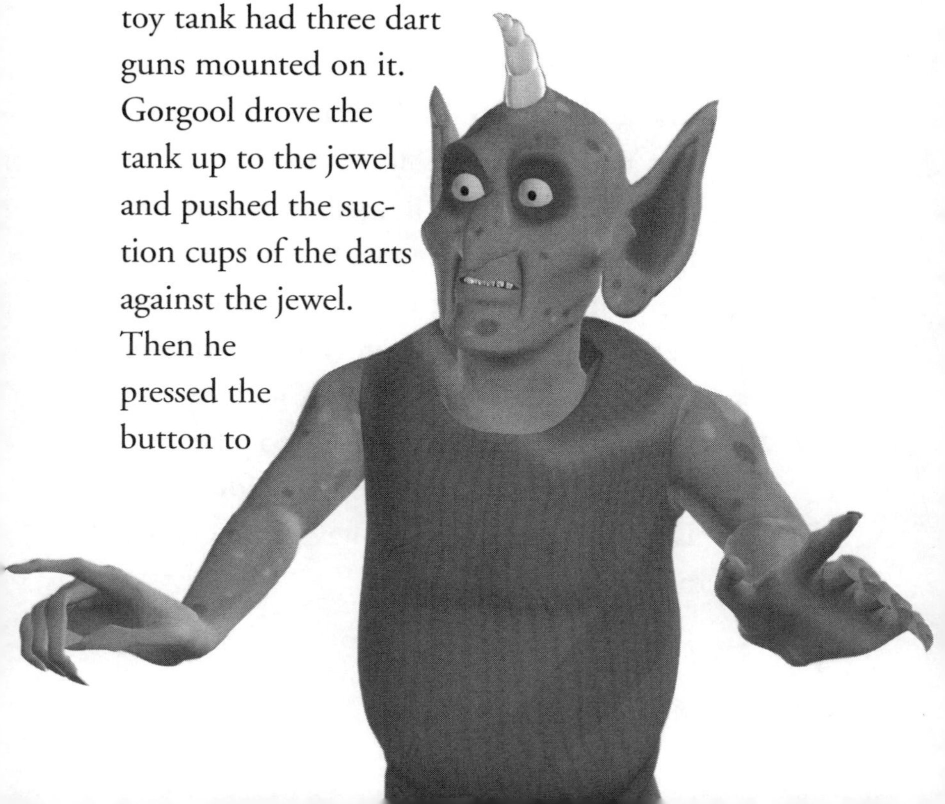

Suddenly, an idea came to him. The toy tank had three dart guns mounted on it. Gorgool drove the tank up to the jewel and pushed the suction cups of the darts against the jewel. Then he pressed the button to raise the dart guns. The tiny guns strained against the weight of the jewel, but finally the jewel was flipped into the air and onto the back of the tank.

"Perfect!" said Gorgool. "Now all I need is the *Book of Spells*. It's in this room somewhere."

And there it was – high atop a bookshelf.

"Curses!" he muttered. How could he possibly get up there?

As Gorgool glared in frustration, Tracy was flying up the stairs to see what was making all the noise. She held onto the banister as she floated to the second floor. Her feet barely touched the ground.

"Um . . . Aunt Dolores? Are you up here?" she called. There was no answer and that made Tracy glad. She let go of the banister and flew the rest of the way. "I've got to reverse this spell before Aunt Dolores sees that I'm having a gravity problem."

Tracy peeked into her bedroom and was shocked to see that the Jewel of Fenrath was gone! She was wondering who might have taken it when there was a loud crash of thunder. Seconds later, all the lights went out. Tracy screamed in surprise.

Aunt Dolores heard her niece screaming and knew there was more trouble. She called out, "Hang tight, Tracy. I'll save you!"

Oh no! thought Tracy. I don't need saving; I need to get my feet on the floor.

Tracy flew into her room and tried to hide. She couldn't let Aunt Dolores see her this way!

Aunt Dolores clumped up the stairs until she reached the doorway to Tracy's bedroom. She turned on her flashlight and pointed it around the room. Where was Tracy? Aunt Dolores finally spotted her niece lying on the curtain rod over the window.

"What the heck are you doing up there?" asked Aunt Dolores.

"Um . . . looking for Warren?" said Tracy, hoping that she sounded convincing.

"Good!" said Aunt Dolores. "Now don't worry about the lights. I'm heading down to the basement to fiddle with the fuse box."

"No! You can't!" said Tracy. She knew that the Monster was hiding in the basement. She thought fast. "I'm, uh, scared, I think. I mean, if you leave, that monster might get me!"

"Don't get your knickers in a twist, hon," said Aunt Dolores. She had a fondness for old-fashioned expressions. "The monster isn't going to get you on MY beat!" With that, Aunt Dolores turned and left Tracy floating over the window.

Aunt Dolores went quickly down the two flights of stairs. The lights were still off and it was pitch black. Using her flashlight, she found the fuse box and started working on it. Hearing a noise over her shoulder, she turned.

"Halt! Who's there?"

She peered into the darkness. Was somebody really there? Aunt Dolores aimed her flashlight at the floor and moved it until the beam came to a big, blue foot. Raising the flashlight beam, she stared right at the face of the Pickford monster!

For a moment, both were frozen in fear. Then the Monster realized he had to do something, fast. I'll have to scare Aunt Dolores, he thought. The Monster rolled his eyes back in his head and stretched out his arms, trying to look as scary as possible. He lumbered forward slowly, waving his arms like he had seen Frankenstein do in old movies.

"Just put your hands up and come along quietly," said Aunt Dolores.

Fat chance, thought the Monster. He kept moving forward, as scary as only a large blue Frankenstein could be.

Aunt Dolores nervously backed up as the Monster approached her. Not realizing it, Aunt Dolores stepped into Tom Patterson's tool cabinet.

The Monster saw his chance. He quickly slammed the doors of the tool cabinet and locked her in.

"Hey, you're under arrest! Do you hear me, Monster Man? You're dealing

with a police officer!" yelled Aunt Dolores from inside the cabinet.

The Monster knew exactly whom he was dealing with. He also knew that he and Tracy had only a little time before their parents would come home. Somehow they had to fix all this by then.

In the dark kitchen, the Monster slammed into Tracy.

"Where's Aunt Dolores?" asked Tracy.

"I locked her in Dad's tool cabinet downstairs."

"Oh, great," Tracy groaned, then asked, "Can you sneeze yet?"

"No," said her brother. "The allergy medicine still hasn't worn off. And why are you still flying? I thought you were going to reverse the spell."

"The jewel's missing!" Tracy exclaimed. "I can't do any magic without it!"

"What are we going to do now?" the Monster asked.

"Leave it to me," Tracy said. "I'm the babysitter and I'm in charge." There was confidence in her voice, but a sinking feeling in her heart.

Chapter 7

Up in Tracy's room, Gorgool was still trying to get the *Book of Spells* off the top of the bookcase. He had the toy tank's dart guns pointing straight up and his ball resting on the end of the darts. But Gorgool was still a long way from the book.

His servant was still outside the house. The storm had stopped, so he figured it was safe to come out of hiding. Carefully he climbed the ladder up to Tracy's window. When he looked inside, he saw Gorgool coming down from one of his jumps.

"Master! You're falling!" wailed the servant. He leaped into the room to catch Gorgool.

Unfortunately, the servant's aim wasn't good on the best of days. And this hadn't been a very good day at all. The servant missed and landed on top of Gorgool. The two of them slammed into the bookshelf and fell to the floor.

Gorgool was groggy from the impact. The servant was afraid his master would be angry again.

"Master? Are you okay?" he asked.

"No, idiot! You nearly crushed me!"

"I was trying to save you!" said the servant.

"I don't need your help, you fool!" said Gorgool angrily. "I got the jewel back myself, no thanks to you."

His servant was heartbroken. "Please, Mighty Gorgool. Please don't fire me again," he begged.

"Give me one good reason why I shouldn't!" scowled Gorgool.

The servant blinked frantically as he tried to come up with a reason.

"I . . . uh . . . because . . . well, uh, I think . . . uh, maybe . . ."

Try as hard as he might, the servant couldn't think of any reasons. He picked up a book that had fallen off the bookcase and started hitting himself on the head with it.

"Think! Think! Think!" he yelled as he hit his head.

Gorgool's jaw dropped. He couldn't believe it. His idiot servant had the book he needed right in his hand.

"That's it!" he yelled. "The *Book of Spells*!"

The servant stopped hitting himself and looked at the book. "Hey, it is! Does this mean I'm not fired any more?"

"I suppose so," said Gorgool with a sigh.

The servant was as happy as a puppy dog. He picked up Gorgool's ball and hugged it.

"Oh thank you, Master! Thank you. Thank you. Thank you."

"Stop it," said Gorgool. "This is no time for affection, you fool! I hear someone coming. Quickly, out the window!"

The servant tossed the *Book of Spells* and the jewel out the window into the backyard. Then he started to climb down the ladder.

"Aren't you forgetting something?" yelled Gorgool from the floor.

"Uh, what?" asked the servant.

"Me, idiot. Pick me up right now . . . and don't forget this toy tank!"

The servant had just made it back to the ladder with Gorgool and the tank when the Monster arrived!

Chapter 8

In the basement, Aunt Dolores was still stuck in the tool cabinet. There was a screwdriver pushing into her back and the blade of a saw up against her leg. But those were the least of her problems. The Pickford monster was upstairs in the house – and had kidnapped poor Warren.

She had to get out and catch that monster!

Dolores looked around with her flashlight. Up above her shoulder, she spotted a battery-powered drill. It took a while to find a drill bit, but then Dolores set to work. Moments later, the cabinet doors fell open and Aunt Dolores stepped out. "I'm coming, Warren!" she yelled. "I'll be there in a second." Then she went straight for the fuse box to fix the lights.

Up in Tracy's room, the last thing the Monster needed was Aunt Dolores. He was busy wrestling with the very large servant at the window – monster versus servant. The Monster's body was big, but a little clumsy. The servant might not be smart, but he sure was tough to hold onto.

Suddenly, the lights came on. From the basement, Aunt Dolores yelled, "Tracy! Have you found Warren yet?"

The Monster looked over his shoulder, worried that his aunt was about to find him. As he turned, the servant pushed the ladder away from the building. The ladder wobbled and tipped. The servant tried desperately to keep it balanced, but it was no use. The ladder fell onto the grass. Shortly after, the servant, Gorgool and the toy tank came tumbling down. They made an enormous pile on the back lawn.

"Warren, quick, get out before Aunt Dolores gets here," Tracy ordered.

"But they've got the jewel!" said her monster brother.

"Don't worry about those two. I'll take care of them! Remember, I'm in charge," declared Tracy.

The Monster wondered if his sister was still in her right mind, but he did what she asked. He ran out of the room and Tracy stood at the window, looking down over the backyard. She took a deep breath and flew out the window into the night.

In the upstairs hallway, the Monster and Aunt Dolores ran into each other.

"Yikes!" screamed Dolores. "I mean, stop in the name of the Pickford Police."

The Monster had no intention of stopping. He did a quick about-face and ran into Tracy's room. Aunt Dolores was close behind – but not close enough.

When Aunt Dolores entered, the Monster was nowhere to be seen.

"What the . . . ? Where in the heck did he go? He's got to be in here," said a confused Aunt Dolores.

As she poked around the room, the Monster peeked out from behind the bedroom door. He tried to sneak out while Aunt Dolores's back was turned, but she turned around. The Monster reacted quickly and managed to get right behind her. He was as close to her as a shadow!

"Don't try to escape the Pickford Police," Aunt Dolores said. "We always get our man."

Actually, thought the Monster, it's the Mounties who always get their man. Besides, Warren was a monster – not a

man – and Dolores was no Mountie. She wasn't even aware that the Monster was right behind her.

"I mean, a seven-foot-tall monster just can't vamoose!" Aunt Delores sat back on what she thought was a very comfortable chair. "No way he could disappear. This here's a real puzzler," she said to herself.

Aunt Dolores stroked her chin and then started drumming her fingers. She wondered why her comfortable chair felt a little strange . . . a little warm. When she looked down, she had the answer.

"Yaaaaaah!" she yelled.

Aunt Delores wasn't sitting on a chair, she was sitting right on the Pickford monster!

The Monster jumped up, frightened by her scream, tossing Aunt Dolores to the floor. Then he ran from the room.

Dolores scrambled to her feet and dashed into the hallway. She got a glimpse of the monster's foot going up the attic stairs. Aunt Dolores was sure she had her man . . . or monster, as the case may be.

"Ah, ha!" she yelled. "I've got you now! Your heiny's miney!"

Chapter 9

Tracy flew through the night air, chasing Gorgool and his servant across the backyard. Gorgool drove the toy tank with the Jewel of Fenrath. The servant carried the *Book of Spells* in his very large hands.

"Stop!" Tracy yelled. "You'll never get away with this!"

The servant looked over his shoulder and saw Tracy hovering in front of the full moon.

"M-m-master! It's a witch!" said the frightened servant.

"Don't be a fool," said Gorgool. "It's just that annoying girl. Luckily, I'm ready to deal with her!"

Gorgool shifted his ball on top of the

tank. With a sudden bounce, he fired all three darts at Tracy.

The darts bounced off Tracy quite harmlessly. "Sticks and stones may break my bones, but toy darts will never hurt me," she said triumphantly.

"No one can stop Gorgool! No one!" he yelled.

Tracy disagreed. She flew into a nearby tree and came out with her arms full of apples. "Bombs away!" she yelled. Then she began throwing the apples at the servant. Tracy's aim was excellent. The servant dropped the *Book of Spells* as he tried to protect his head.

"The book, you fool!" Gorgool yelled.

"But, Master," the servant whined, "the apples hurt my head!"

"Your head might as well be a block of wood!" shouted Gorgool. "Now fight back!"

The servant managed to catch an apple and throw it back at Tracy, but she dodged it easily. Tracy responded with an apple barrage! She landed several direct hits, driving the servant away. Then it was time to direct her attack against his ill-tempered master!

Gorgool was driving the toy tank around the yard, zigzagging to avoid Tracy's apples.

Tracy grew frustrated. This time she wasn't going to miss! She took the biggest, juiciest apple she had and took careful aim.

"Three, two, one . . . bomb's away!" she yelled.

This time Tracy's aim was perfect. The apple smashed on impact, spreading applesauce all over Gorgool's ball. Gorgool couldn't see!

Blinded by the applesauce, Gorgool drove the tank wildly through the yard. Which way should he go? He had to get away before he lost the jewel!

Taking a chance, he made the tank go as fast as it could. Since he could hardly see where he was going, all he could do was hope for the best.

What Gorgool needed wasn't hope but a windshield wiper. Soon his tank smashed into a tree and the jewel rolled away.

Tracy did a victory dance in the air. Then she dived towards the ground. In a single graceful move, she grabbed both the book and jewel.

"I knew I'd get the hang of flying sooner or later," she said proudly.

The servant scooped up Gorgool from where he had rolled on the lawn. Then he ran down the street, afraid of what Tracy might do next.

Gorgool could hardly contain his rage. "You fool! We were so close! How could you have lost the book and jewel again?"

"Me, Master?"

"Yes, you idiot. It's all your fault!"

The servant could only scratch his head. It seemed to him that it was mostly Gorgool's fault, but he decided to say nothing. After all, Gorgool might fire him again.

Tracy laughed as she watched the two of them running away. "Never underestimate a babysitter," she declared.

Chapter 10

In the attic, Aunt Dolores was feeling more confident as she continued her search for the monster. "The jig's up, Monster. Come out now and we'll go easy on ya!" she said.

The Monster was stuffed inside a wardrobe. He was scared. He didn't want to be discovered by anyone, certainly not by Aunt Dolores. After all, Dolores was a police officer. The Monster might end up in jail. What would his parents say if they had to bail out their son – a large blue monster?

While the Monster was thinking about these dire possibilities, he felt something tickle his nose. He turned to find an old feather boa. It must have belonged to his great-grandmother.

Then he realized his nose was tickling a lot! Hey, he thought to himself, it seems my allergy medicine is wearing off.

The Monster wiggled his nose against the boa to help the sneeze along. "Ah . . . ah . . . ah-choo!"

Aunt Dolores heard the sneeze and zeroed in on the wardrobe. "You've had your warning, Monster! I'm coming in!" she said.

Dolores grabbed the wardrobe door and pulled it open. But there was no monster inside! "Warren?" said a surprised Aunt Dolores.

"Oh, hello, Aunt Dolores," Warren replied.

"You little scamp," his aunt replied. "I've been looking everywhere for you!"

Warren had his answer all ready. "The thunder scared me, so I came up here to hide."

Dolores looked around the attic. "What about the monster? Where'd he go? Did you see him?"

"Um, no," said Warren. "Not since I've been up here. What kind of monster was he? Red? Fluffy?"

Dolores was confused. "Blue," she told him. "Blue and big and crafty. And it looks like he escaped the long arm of the law again!"

"Looks that way, doesn't it?" Warren agreed. It was all he could do to keep a straight face.

"Come on, let's get you back to your sister. I've got to go down to the station and file a report."

Aunt Dolores headed for the stairs. As Warren followed her, he spotted Tracy flying outside the attic window. Tracy smiled and held up the book and jewel. Warren gave her a thumbs-up and followed Aunt Dolores down the stairs.

Chapter 11

Things finally calmed down at the Patterson house. Aunt Dolores was gone. Gorgool and his servant had run away. Tracy reversed her flying spell and Warren was himself again.

Tracy and Warren sat back on the living room couch and munched on popcorn. They never did get to the part where the swamp monster ate Alabama, but Warren was glad. That kind of thing always scared him.

Shortly after midnight, their parents arrived home. Johnny the ghost came in with them, even if their parents couldn't see him. Johnny was smiling. Somehow he'd gotten an autograph from the world-famous singer!

"How was Umberto Ungulessi?" Warren asked his parents.

"Oh, he was fantastic," said their mother. "He's just as handsome in real life as he is on TV."

"But not as handsome as me, eh?" Dad asked.

"No, dear, of course not," she said. "It's just that you don't sing quite as well as he does."

Tom Patterson just smiled. "What about you kids?" he asked. "Any problems?"

Warren turned to Tracy to see what she would say. Tracy crossed her legs, put her hands behind her head and smiled. "Nothing we couldn't handle," she said proudly. "After all, Dad, I was in charge!"

The End

www.monsterbymistake.com

- ❑ experience a 3-D on line adventure
- ❑ preview the next episodes
- ❑ play lots of cool games
- ❑ join the international fan club (it's free)
- ❑ test your knowledge with the trivia quiz
- ❑ visit a full library of audio and video clips
- ❑ enter exciting contests to win GREAT PRIZES
- ❑ surf in English or French

TOP SECRET!

Sneak Preview of New Monster By Mistake Episodes

Even more all-new monster-iffic episodes of Monster by Mistake are on the way in 2003 and 2004! Here's an inside look at what's ahead for Warren, Tracy and Johnny:

- It promises to be a battle royale when a superstar wrestler comes to town and challenges the Monster to a match at the Pickford arena.
- There's a gorilla on the loose in Pickford, but where did it come from? It's up to the Monster, Tracy and Johnny to catch it and solve the mystery.
- When making deliveries for a bakery, Warren discovers who robbed the Pickford Savings and Loan. Can the Monster stop the robbers from getting away?
- Warren, Tracy and Johnny visit Fenrath, the home to Gorgool, the Book of Spells and the Jewel. In Fenrath, they discover who imprisoned Gorgool in the ball and what they must do in order to restore order to this magical kingdom.

MONSTER By Mistake! Videos

Six Monster by Mistake home videos are available and more are on the way.

Each video contains 2 episodes and comes with a special Monster surprise!

Only $9.99 each.

Monster by Mistake & Entertaining Orville
1-55366-130-3

Fossel Remains & Kidnapped 1-55366-131-1

Monster a Go-Go & Home Alone 1-55366-132-X

Billy Caves In & Tracy's Jacket 1-55366-202-4

Campsite Creeper & Johnny's Reunion
1-55366-201-6

Gorgools' Pet & Jungle Land
1-55366-200-8

About the people who brought you this book

Located in Toronto, Canada, **Cambium** has been producing quality family entertainment since 1982. Some of their best known shows are *Sharon Lois and Bram's The Elephant Show*, *Eric's World*, and of course, *Monster By Mistake*!

Catapult Productions in Toronto wants to entertain the whole world with computer animation. Now that we've entertained you, there are only 5 billion people to go!

Mark Mayerson grew up loving animated cartoons and now has a job making them. *Monster By Mistake* is the first TV show he created.

Paul Kropp is an author, editor and educator. His work includes young adult novels, novels for reluctant readers, and the bestselling *How to Make Your Child a Reader for Life*.